Richard Ford

VINTAGE **FORD**

Richard Ford was born in Jackson, Mississippi, in 1944. After graduating from high school, he left Mississippi to attend Michigan State University and went on for graduate work at the University of California at Irvine. Ford completed his first novel, *A Piece of My Heart*, in 1976, which, along with his subsequent novels, *The Ultimate Good Luck* (1981), *The Sportswriter* (1986), and his collection of short stories, *Rock Springs* (1987), earned him an Award in Literature and the Award for Merit in the Novel from the American Academy and Institute of Arts and Letters in 1989. Ford received further acclaim for his novels, *Wildlife* (1990) and *Independence Day* (1995), a sequel to *The Sportswriter* and the first book ever to win both the Pulitzer Prize and the PEN/Faulkner Award. His most recent publications are the collections of short stories, *Women with Men* (1997) and *A Multitude of Sins* (2001), for which he became the recipient in 2001 of the PEN/Malamud Award for excellence in short fiction. Along with his other various accolades, Ford has been elected a member of the American Academy and of the French Order of Arts and Letters.